The Diamond

"by"

Robert B. Davis II

ISBN: 978-0-9978464-2-3 (ebook)
ISBN: 978-0-9978464-1-6 (print)

Contents

The painting
Of the painter painting
Himself painting his painting
Of himself on himself

Here is only a tribute,
We the attributes of God

—Today—

Long you may live

But never will you be apart from This

...

The Old Master

"From the beginning the end is known," the Old Master croaks, "the river and the basin are an illusion. With the Vajrayana it passes—the breath of God through all."

We sat around him listening. "Sit how you like to sit," he would say, "as long as you feel it." I had found some time ago—it seemed long ago to me—that sitting crossed legged, let alone in lotus, didn't agree with my legs. Since giving leave to their shape and limitations I had found several comfortable and powerfully grounding ways of sitting.

The Old Master was like that. Nothing was required. It was said, if you will recall, that the Buddha sat in the lotus position *because it felt natural.* That was the position that his legs lent themselves to, so he chose to sit as such. Long have been remembered and recorded the dimensions of the Buddha; what his feet are like, the shape of his head, etc. Thus when studying in that vein—thinking that form signified achievement—it seemed imperative to be able to sit in full lotus. How else could one be enlightened? The Old Master showed me I was thinking backwards; proper sitting—enlightened sitting—follows feeling, flows from the achievement. It finds the place of no resistance. Get into your seat as water flows to the sea and you will be sitting in the ocean of enlightenment. "Finish," he said, "then follow through."

I cannot tell you who the Old Master is, only what he is. He is a storyteller. And he has a knack for telling just that story that you need to hear. You may want to hear it, each word may thrill your ears and expand your mind, or you may not, and it may bore you. But you will find that it stays with you and reveals itself unbidden. In that way the Old Master knows your future, in that way he lives inside your mind. His stories, then, are told to himself—the He that lives in you—and he only ever awakes himself.

"Stories are not invented," said the Old Master, "they are discovered. They do not belong to the writer or the speaker, they belong to themselves. Some merely know the way to unveil what is already there; it is brought to light for they— the light—go and find it. All is there, on the page and as the page, but how it is molded and what is shown comes through confluence of paper, pen, and writer—only one of which we normally identify with."

To us the Old Master spoke. He opened his mouth and his mouth was the universe, and we, the world, the word on his tongue.

—To be in a Tree—

Once in a tree

It seems absurd that it is considered absurd,

Or simply not considered at all,

"Superpowers" will not save you from monotony

You must save yourself from the illusion

Then you will find yourself in the arms of that Tree

And, too, as the wind that is with it

…

The Frog Stands Forth

"Around your base scuttles the scorpion, over your feet and around your heels in a figure eight pattern. Out the back of your head soars an eagle, its wing tips fringe your ears. But there is a frog in your belly. Stay with the frog for he has a song." So the Old Master said to me. "The eagle has a song," I said. "The eagle has a cry," the Old Master remarked, "His cry is high and mighty, and calls many aloft to his eyrie, but a song is better still. And you need not climb as high with the frog; you need only face the night."

"When the three are gathered, two are at odds," He said, "the scorpion raises its claws and flexes its tail. It knows it is low, and it sinks lower. So much time down here and it knows the ground well. This is its best defense, its menace in answer to its fear of inferiority as the eagle swoops down. 'The eagle is mighty indeed,' the scorpion thinks, 'it commands what is so high and far, sees all, and travels quickly and at will. It will surely overtake me and it will easily conquer me, so I must be both dangerous and still. It is times like these when a poisonous reputation has been worth the cultivation.'

'The scorpion is vile and low,' thinks the great bird, 'Each time I fly by he waves for my attention with his sinister claws and threatens the thrust of his poisoned sting. It might be well to do this land a favor and rid him from it, but should his sting but clip my wing I could be in trouble indeed; though I would still win the fight, who would be here then to watch over the wind in these treacherous nights?'"

"Each of the pair sees the third and shares a common thought, 'Here is a good and easy meal, how foolishly does it stand so exposed.' Eagle in the sky, scorpion in his dune, but the frog sees only the sun and the moon. Whether night or day he has the same thing to say, and he croaks his thesis gladly, delighting in the mad melody. 'Hark!' he bellows from his bowels, 'the water knows the way!' It is his sound that reveals his crown. It thuds against the fog, rises under bridges, and rolls by the reeds. Always it takes its lead from water, and skips like stones in harmonious tune."

This became one of the Old Master's most famous stories. Gypsies and wild healers for years would quote his allegory for remedies. Many a sick traveler was coaxed into the swallowing of a frog. But more congenially, after such a time that folks needed to be reminded of meaning through expansion, parents began to tell their children that this frog was once a man. And that this man became learned in wizardry and became an animagus. "A man of great power," they said he was, "and of all the animals he could become, in that moment he chose to become a frog. For it was only with such a deep song of substance as the frog's that he could avert this fight between old friends."

"And," they would say, "we are all one people, so this man is you my child, and you are a frog!" And with that they would make a great surprising croak and the children would squeal with delight, and their parents would kiss them good night. As they left the room and turned to close the door, they would speak a few words more, "you can be anything you want in this life my child, and that right soon, even a frog. To anything you might turn in this next moment, but it is in love you are beholden, so it is you are golden. My child you are golden."

—The Lord's Eternal Art—
I once knew a spaceman who said
You are a sad, strange little man.
J-O-Y! Joy!
Joy to the world I am a toy,
The feeling is whole in your heart
We are

...

It Flows

Once I came to the Old Master and said that Eternity was like a river, for so I had seen it. He laughed and said, "Oh no, how wrong you are! Eternity is the basin, the river's very bed; that is the place of the Godhead that does not move and we are its flowing dreams."

I went back to my meditations and tried to find this stillness. Later that day another student who had been standing by earlier came to the master and said, "I have seen it! Eternity is the basin, and we flowing through!" But the master laughed again and said, "How foolish of you, don't you know the truth? Eternity runs like a river through this," waving his hand, "its statuesque creation, and so are we enlivened."

"Master," I objected, "you have now given two conflicting answers, we are used to your paradoxes but we are seeking to express true visions we have had, how do you answer us so?"

"You are lost in conflict," said he, "enamored with it.

Where is there any conflict? My advice was, first of all given to two separate individuals about two separate visions, to each I emphasized the opposing side which they were so excited to forget. And further there still would be no conflict had I offered them both to one of you concerning subsequent so-called visions. You are blind and have no vision until you understand that the river and the basin are one and the same."

"To emphasize the activity, the movement, the male, the exhale, the playful river of consciousness dancing around its monument is to raise the left hand." And he did so, bent ninety degrees at the elbow, palm out. His right arm extended, bent down at the elbow, palm facing back. "To emphasize the passive, the stillness, the female, the inhale, the loving and benevolent presence is to raise the right hand," he reversed his arms, "Both grow out of I."

"How then should we speak of it?" I asked. "It cannot be done comprehensively." He responded, "So the ancients used empty words and titles—pointing words. After a while all that can be said of it is, 'There is this Radiance.' Then further, 'There is This.' Then, 'There is' or the 'I am'. Then, 'Is' which is 'I'. But silence says more."

"Symbolism is superior to explication," said the Old Master, "How shall I explain this? Words make sense only once you've learned sense—escaped the prison of your mind. The symbols of Eternity—the Eye, the Yin and Yang, the Cross, the Diamond—endure and yet contain movement. Nay it is because they contain movement that they endure."

—Leaves—
Air run through water to take shape
Splayed to the tune of sunlight
But such is any Earthly blossom
And so we too

This Sky

One morning the Old Master was out walking and singing, "Love, Love, Love." I came to him and asked, "Why, Master, do you sing of This Sky and not this Earth? Surely you have taught me it gets one nowhere to go off flying with the Eagle."

He turned and said, "This earth on which you think you walk is a matter of great myth and legend. Earth alone may encompass some general ideas of varying surroundings, but *this* Earth is quite an illusion, though you see it clearly by the light of day. All you have is presence in this moment, and it stretches out as infinite radiance. Where is this flat or rolling, climbing or falling plane you will call the Earth?"

"In truth you will find no lines, only circles. Any perceived line, including this Earth is but a great circle truncated by the mind. Can you not see how it grows out of you, and that you are but an extension of it?"

"What is more, you have delineated—created—the

Earth, and now you want to distinguish it from others or refer to it as the constant between two. If the sage walks in the foot prints of the lost man do they walk the same path? If the lost man follows the light steps of the sage do they tread the same substance? Some say yes, some say no. The ground, the Earth beneath you is as uncertain as turbid water, and yet we have long clung to it as a symbol of what is enduring. This is not wrong, for much of our time we need the symbol of an anchor, and for this we need the ignorance of a constant. But look into what is constant and you will unveil this illusion, best then you should be ready to set sail."

There are many things humans keep around and yet are afraid to look into, this I have found to be true. On the same day he showed me my wings, the Old Master educated me about poo.

"There is an ancient friendship between human beings and shit," He began, "though for the most part we would deny it. The rituals and habits of humans change over time, but this one is common to nearly all even across their entire span of time, and by it do many other beings define the human form and realm. Mundane is this spectrum called where shit is kept around, and many out there look down even on those who know not it is their choice."

"We have chosen this place, this life here on Earth along with all that entails. Strife we usually confine to the withdrawal of our goals before us, and we make tales to help ourselves persevere. But strife comes too in the denial of what is true, this is called repression. Often psychiatry deals with the repression of impulses and emotions about all things taboo, but rarely if ever have I heard them teach one how to live with their poo. We think we've got it down. Gradually we teach children control of their bodily organism, then we teach them proper refinement in keeping their dumps quiet. The commode kept white and clean, the porcelain throne perfected in its efficacy at whisking our filth away. An accord we have struck where we grant this friend his leisure to stay part of our lives, so long as he takes on the moniker of what is low and defiled and departs quickly after his, hopefully peaceful, exile."

"Of course we have strong secondary incentive to keep him around, for we love to eat and in this world it is explained that those go together. But look into the infinite and see, amidst all possibility, this is certainly untrue. Each part of life is kept around by our own will, and if life is a pleasure, secretly we must all enjoy our poo."

"Now," said the Old Master knowingly, "there will be two inappropriate reactions to such an accusation from the ego which is unwilling to face it. The first will be disgust and mistrust. Fasts may be undertaken, one may even, God willing, achieve that state of livelihood called the breatharian. An obsession with diet to make one's shits sweet, small and quiet is not at all the way to go. This is to pursue denial and to attempt to forget that this horrible process exists. Let me tell you this now so you will know, one cannot part forever from anything without giving it love. If looked on from above, and eschewed in disgust, down on you someday far ahead your friend will return, remembering what you said."

"The second reaction will be overcompensation, pleasure immoderate sought in sensation. This shit, and with it all things labeled low, will be lauded and elevated. The man who is free from fear of death runs not from it, nor to meet it. To charge in wild denial, overcome with emotive waves, into the face of fear is the essence of succumbing to it. With either action you give it power and reality. It is not necessary or wise to love shit as one loves one's other friends. Each has their form dictating their proper norm. In the end all one must do is accept the presence of poo, together with the knowledge that it is here by attention; that it is your intention to be in this life a being in and of a world that shits. Sit on that white throne for the time allotted; accept even the irony of the created sterile ritual. Know it is part of the story and freedom will be yours, surely."

—Q & A—
If I see Diamonds,
Aren't there Diamonds in my Eyes?
Apertures
Of
Eternity
Diamonds are made in
Imitation
Of
Eyes

The Vajrayana

A man once came to the Old Master and asked how to attain the infinite. "I have sat by the river in silence, I have tempered the heat of burning fire with non-action, yet my quest goes on." He looked to the Old Master who said, "A change of perspective, a flame and rises the phoenix. His tales are mountain rivers, his wings are fiery stone. He lies over distant homeland, but have the courage to go and stand there and you shall find your throne." The man bowed and left in silence.

The man had journeyed long to consult the Old Master, and long was his road back home. There is no need to detail his hardships, for always the traveler has many. Steadfastly he weathered them and continued on. He came to his valley home at sunset and watched the golden blood of life kiss the peaks of the mountains. His bed lay already in shadow. He would not rest this night but would climb until sunrise that he might be first with the mountains to receive the Grace that next day.

The moon was full and bright and he was followed by his shadow through half the night. Then the stars swirling overhead faded and the moon dissipated. These apophatic absences marked the dark clouds descent. But he continued up into the black night, crawling with arms and legs over boulders and beside ravines. The night mocked him, "How tall you stand in the day, how confident you are then that the wind won't carry you away. But now you bend as if gravity is no longer your friend. Even the ruthless Earth it seems throws up stones in your path." But the man had journeyed far and in his heart he held the stars, the river of his childhood, and the fire of his home and wife, so he listened not to the night and stumbled on to the heights still out of sight.

Then a deep shade loomed up in his path and he cowered before its towering limbs. Down the hill swept the wind, and as it passed through he laughed. He heard the branches sway and he knew this tree, it marked the near end of his journey. The highest tree, last of the green crown around that grey peak—though all was grey now.

Then on back of the wind came the rain and he started on again. Up to the very peak, his bones were cold and his limbs were weak. He stood at the summit and felt the hissing rain pelt the last of his strength away. It was cold and he still had the climb down. He would surely get sick. "If such a price I must pay to feel myself this way," for though alone and unseen he felt free, "then let it be. I am close to home and there I might come soon even with much difficulty still. Then I may have time to be ill."

Then the diving valley of night on all sides of his new height swirled around the peak and rushed through his mind. The mountain would not hold him, the darkness would tip him and he would fall, fall into the depths of night forever beyond sight. "It is death I see," he spoke again to the air, "he is in my eye, am I in his? If clear his vision is of me then surely he will strike, and who would I then be to deny my clear mortality? If this is my time, and surely it seems so, then take me; let us go."

When he had spoken thus and looked into the night all at once was bright. In that moment the man saw himself alight, and so too the valley and the mountains in the receding night. The rain was a pattern of suspended jewels and each drop he visited and saw in it reflected the infinite.

What the mountains saw in that mighty flash was the clash of lightning upon the earth, passing through a man. He stood alone and for that moment reached up from the peak and touched the sky as the sky descended into his eye. Then it was dark again, and that strange silhouette passed like all others. But for him it did not pass and he stretched out across forever at last. In such place as that no-space, one is finally released from confinement. There he saw all in alignment. In that moment was revealed forever the ever present without need for refinement, and ever after the moments that passed he laughed and saw they resided in the moment which lasts. To those who came to him for teaching he said only this, "A feeling runs together with—as—the current of immediacy. Go see what it is, then you too will tell it on the mountain, over the hills, and everywhere. For thence goes its course, and it you already follow."

The Old Master heard through the wind this man's tale and related it to us. We delighted to think that even now we sat in that moment, that somewhere in that light beyond the night—perhaps in one of the rain drops or encircled in billowing clouds—he looked at us from his height.

—We Are His—
The wind, the wind
Hail to thee!
The almighty sweeping through,
Bringing forward the new
By echo through the trees
It passes subtly
Soft on your skin
And engenders deep within
A chance to recall again

...

The Breath of God

Once I heard a quote from Jung, "Show me a sane man and I shall cure him." I went to the Old Master and inquired about this saying. "Sanity is a shallow basin," he said, "and insanity at its zenith is this belief in so called 'sanity'."

"So we are all insane, even you and I?" I asked. "Absolutely barking," he said, "howling mad the lot of you! But me? I am madness." He smiled. "Think about this as you sit here in conversation with yourself," he continued, "it is within infinite possibility that you are completely mistaken in your understanding of all things and wrong in every action at every moment of your life. That is not to say that this could be the case; it is the case. Here, now you play the categorical fool with no hope of escape. You may see the irony in your every move, the fallacy of every thought but even that acknowledgement is a foolish thing for you to do about your foolishness. This is part of you forever. If you ask 'How shall I live?' in your abjection have you not already embarked on a course? The question need only be asked once, and it was asked at the beginning, all that follows is your answer."

We who had heard went on with our answers that day. We sat near the water, where it is always best to sit, and two near me were discussing their past. In their words I felt the tumult of uncertainty, the rise of hopes and falls of regrets and the general noise of that nonsensical speech which whisks life by under toe even as it seeks to pin something down. It was then that the wind embraced me. The words I was hearing I stopped understanding and the feeling of wind overtook my soul. My skin became the shell of the well which was my soul and the wind stirred at my surface just enough to show me where the stillness was.

My head was brought to my knees as I closed off the senses, and as that last door fell in place, restoring the circle that was me, suddenly it was not me. Emanating from depths unfathomable silence passed through this form like a wave. Clearly—I cannot express how clearly—this form and all I have ever called 'me' showed its thinness. A hologram it seemed, a projection suspended in the topmost layer of transient substance. With such experience, though it seems it hardly need have been reinforced, came the soft intuitive message, "So far are you beyond all this."

The wave passed from top to bottom and moved easily but passed soon. Yet the gravity of its truth made these few moments into lifetimes of peace. My head had just rested a moment before rising again and the conversation beside me continued as though the world had not just fallen into silence, as if God had not just passed perceptibly through his creation.

Listen to the wind, it passes easily through you and visits your soul. If you two are in tune you will hear the wind's true spirit. It is laughter—Joy in motion—the first incarnation of motion in the silence, rolling over substance. Profundity beyond measure, its message recalled with pleasure, but never truly grasped for it exalts, "To Be!"

It is helpful to see that just as you can personify emotions—here is anger, there sorrow, here happiness—so as to stand apart from them though you sense them and their presence is known, you can personify perception too. It and all its construction—everything you fear and hold dear—returns to the same peaceful void. This I know because to me the wind revealed that I am just a show.

—Groundless, Boundless—
You are the rainbow
Incarnate, surfing cosmic
Waves of I—yourSelf

. . .

The Tree

There are only two possibilities with death: release or transport to where you need to be.

Seated peacefully the Old Master prepared for his passing. "For the people," he said to us around, "let them know that 'Do not' is not the will of God. God says, 'Live' and we are contained therein, and only by He is such possible." He paused for a moment and we sat in silence and waited.

"Not as a drum have I beaten the Dharma," he said suddenly, "but as the ground under my feet, with laden falls, curious proddings, trippings and stumblings, light dancing, and elated skipping. A life time of cacophony I now leave behind, and like all else the Lord shall harbor it as his own and wind about it and through it notes divine. So it shall be shown but the smallest phrase in his unending song, yet no less than perfect was its placement, and pure love was given as his attention, now I shall achieve the final apprehension."

As he spoke he seemed to glow faintly, and his words seemed to pass out even perceptibly to sight as though laden with Holy light. And when he finished and his turn had come, he passed directly into light. And in the place of his passing—his blooming—there grew a tree.

Quickly it sprang up as if time saw fit to make this season due for ten. This tree sent out six great ballasted roots and at the points where each root dived under the soil there was made a symbol. Every other had the collapsed Eye—the two out looking 'E''s—that is the great 'I' and the other three were given the two pyramids, top and bottom—the diamond—at whose center rests the all seeing eye with its spiraling trails. "On Earth, as it is in Heaven." They said. The trunk of this tree climbed in the center and its bark seemed to flow with water, as if that which was in fought to turn out and that which was out was happy to dive within itself. And they recalled what the Old Master had said, "Many lines make a tree, and each of our lives is one line in the Tree of Life." And so it was said that this tree's branches became invisible as they grew out and stretched onward into the world, and climbed up through our bodies and coned full of electricity as what we call our nervous system. And its roots cut through time like stone and began the Earth itself for its own growing pleasure.

Long did that tree stand—three thousand years some reckoned it—and long was it before the people forgot its true story, and never was it missed as a Holy place. While its story lasted it brought Joy and new life to all who visited, for here was a mark of the infinite upon itself in form they had been taught to see, or which had grown into their vision. And many learned to see such marks more and more around them, until they walked their life through the forest of these affirmations and they danced and rejoiced in the firmament across which their songs spread in resonance with the weave of Being itself.